CRAFTING YOUR PRAYER LIFE

A 58 Day Journey of Prayer,
Mediation, and Reflection

By Maurice Schofield

DEDICATION

To everyone who is striving to do life with a peace of mind, joy, and without fear to pray about everything!

To my family that's grieving, cast your anxieties to the Father & learn from your defining moments with him!

To everyone that will be impacted by this journey, hold on to God! Don't let go of him!

ACKNOWLEDGMENTS

If you are traveling through life with pain, fear, worry, and regret on your shoulders; I encourage you to build and sustain a healthy line of prayer with the creator.

Life will pose with a smile through various situations and circumstances with opportunities to excel or fail at thriving. Yes, you will have your fair share of challenges! Allow God to be your catalyst! He did not place you on this planet to worry but to live abundantly in and through him.

Take this 58-day journey of prayer, mediation, and reflection to transform your worry into burgeoning act of Faith!

INTRODUCTION

One day I wake up worried about everything in my present, past, and future. After starting year 2022, I made up my mind to worry less. I know that I should pray, display patience, follow the guidance of the Holy Spirit, but further understanding was needed. Within the months of February and March I decided to write out my prayers daily. This is how the odd, but even number 58 prayers were crafted!

The goal was not too simple write out my prayers, I wanted to value patience and perseverance even more. I was once empowered to pray about everything, but also remember to look back and tell God Thank You! In this book you will not just see the painted picture of a season of my prayer life, but you will start crafting your story as well while writing out your prayers to God.

The purpose of this literature is to help everyone who is journeying through life and need a boost to advance in payer, mediation, reflection, and reading God's Word for peace. In between every seven days of prayer there are reflection moments to help you recap and allow God to bring to life your own crafted story. Capitalize on your defining moments with the creator, they will help you conquer some life challenges.
Enjoy your journey through all fifty-eight days of Crafting Your Prayer Life!

Pop Quiz:

1. What are you worried about currently?
2. Are you willing to cast it, them, and/or those things to God?
3. Are you ready to gain a peace of mind?

Day 1: There Is A Reason (8 AM)

Father God, thank you for your blessings! Day 32 of the year 2022 has been rewarding! Through the challenges, father, I realize how much I genuinely need your guidance, love, strength, understanding, and zeal that continues to strengthen me to not give up on you! Despite what people have said about my character, roles, purpose, and expressions of who you have crafted me to be, there is still a reason to pray!

Today, Father, I'm asking that you bless my management team, hourly staff, today/tomorrows youth, my brothers/sisters in Christ, my family, my enemies, those who want to see me fail, leadership across the world, those who are on the way to turn their life over to you, those who are thriving daily to live in you, and those who will return to you before it's too late.

I don't know what today will bring, but father, thank you for allowing me to embrace today! I am a little worried about my yesterday, but father, I know that you have me covered. I need your power, love, structured, and sound mind to manage my responsibilities today! No matter the outcome, father, I know that there is a reason! In Jesus Christ's Name, Amen!

Read Philippians 2:1-5

Meditation

_____

_____

_____

_____

Pray To The Father

_____

_____

_____

_____

_____

_____

_____

Day 2: The Unexpected (12:45 PM)

Dear Father, I was worried about how today was going to flow! I cried from many assumptions of yesterday! I fail to trust your process, but today will be awesome! You gave me the energy! You gave me strength! You gave me your attention! You sent a word of encouragement! You relaxed me holistically for the challenges of today! Thank You!

Thanks for preparing me for action! Thanks for your love and protection! Thanks for giving me clear and concise support! Thanks for being my awesome Father!

Today father, I will simply accept the unexpected! I will plan and live by your grace! I will hold up my shoulders and allow my head to rest high! I will seek your ways on this day! I will put myself aside to allow you to add value to your precious creation! In Jesus' Name, Amen!

Read Matthew 6:25-34

Meditation

_____

_____

_____

Cry Out To The Father

_____

_____

_____

Day 3: Don't Lose Your Purpose (1 PM)

Dear Father, you have given me multiple roles and responsibilities! Today I feel empowered! Many around me are struggling! Please help them, father. I've prayed for others! I've prayed for my circumstances! I've prayed about my future! I've encouraged others! Pops, I'm grateful!

On day one, I prayed about my team! Thank you for the boost of joy that you've brought to us! We've improved in operation! More changes to come! Father, thank you for your blessings. As a leader in various capacities, I still need guidance, help, support, encouragement, and discipline. I know you see, hear, and understand the journey you gave me. I will continue!

As you direct my steps today, father, please bless me to prep for the future! You know my desires! You made me unique! You give me a fresh start! Today father, I don't want to lose my purpose in glorifying you! Thank you for the commitment to one gallon a day! Thank you for your dedication to praying to you every day! Thank you for preparing me for the future to become a husband, father, and full-time minister and for the itinerary to where you will take us! Father, thank you for relaxing my mind to remain focused! In Jesus' Name, Amen!

Read Jeremiah 29:11

Meditation

_____

_____

_____

_____

Tell The Father About It

_____

_____

_____

_____

_____

_____

_____

_____

Day 4: Message Received (11:44 PM)

Dear Father, I don't have much to say! One thing that I will express is to thank you for an answered prayer! In Jesus' Name, Amen!

Read Matthew 11:26-30

Meditation

_____

_____

_____

_____

Pray To The Father

_____

_____

_____

Day 5: Take It Back (7:50 PM)

Father God today started great until I decided to look back and do something I said I would never do again! Pops, it hurts! I know you will see me through, but I must let go of the past! My future is waiting on me.

You know my desires! You are building in me a healthy legacy for my family and me to serve you! Father, I'm tired of draining your energy on the thoughts of a relationship that failed! Every time I look back, I feel depleted of strength to press through.

Father God, I need your help to let go and March forward! I know you're prepping me for my beautiful wife, ready to commit to one husband! My wife, who is my ultimate soulmate, helpmate, lover, friend, and yes, father, my ministry twin! I know in due season you will present her to me. A remarkable woman for me to love, share life with, start a family with, nurture, protect, understand, and yes, Father, I will be her best man! Father, as you prepare me for her and her for me, please, pops, help us to do life together regardless of any stormy weather! In Jesus' Name, Amen!

Read 2 Corinthians 12:7-10

Meditation

_____

_____

_____

_____

Share It With The Father

_____

_____

_____

_____

_____

_____

_____

_____

Day 6: Stop Making It Hard (10 PM)

Father God, I see that I continue to make things more complicated by not letting go and allowing you to order my steps! What should I do, pops? How should I do what you need me to do? How do I start what you need me to do? In Jesus' Name, Amen!

Read 1 Corinthians 10: 13

Meditation

_____

_____

_____

_____

_____

The Creator Want You To Share It

Day 7: Change The Story (8 AM)

Father God, thank you for another opportunity to do what's simply right! I failed slightly this morning, but I'm grateful that you picked me up and brushed the dust away. I can see clearly what your Holy Spirit is guiding me to do. I will complete a self-examination! I will write a new reconciliation plan! I will pray to you about everything! I will use your strength! I will walk through this day, understanding your purpose for me! Thanks for being my shepherd! I will dwell with you forever! In Jesus' Name, Amen!

Read Psalm 23:1-6

Meditation

_____

_____

_____

_____

Pray To God About It

_____

_____

_____

_____

_____

_____

_____

Reflection Moments

1. After traveling through the past seven days of your week what have you learned about yourself?

2. What have you learned about your connection with the creator?

3. Take what you have learned to embrace the next seven days of your journey to thrive!

Day 8: Hold On (11:48 PM)

Father God, thanks for the eye-opener! I'm glad to be your servant! I'm so happy about everything you are preparing me to learn, embrace, and demonstrate on my journey with you! Pops today was attractive! Thanks for breathing fresh air into me! Thanks for your blessings, joy, tears, pain, conquered fears, a career, money, a home, food, forgiveness, love, guidance, shelter, ministry, salvation, family, and most importantly, your word!

I felt better today, pops, knowing that you have me covered! I know that every day will be different, and I must focus on one day at a time! Thank you for the complaints, corporate walkthrough, my team, and the journey to hold on through working together! We need each other, and we need you! Please bless us, pops, to not give up on our role & responsibilities! Instead, help everyone to hold on! Please, pops, help my brothers and sisters to hold on! Please, pops, help my family to hold on! In Jesus' Name, Amen!

Read 1 Corinthians 15:58

Meditation

_____

_____

_____

_____

_____

_____

_____

_____

Pray To God About It

_____

_____

_____

_____

_____

_____

_____

_____

_____

_____

_____

_____

Day 9: God, I Love You More (8:57 AM)

Father God, thanks for another day to look up to you! I don't know how you will use me in every detail of my journey today, but I'm ready to be used for your glory. In Jesus' Name, Amen!

Read Matthew 22: 37-39

Meditation

_____

_____

_____

_____

_____

_____

Why Not Tell Him About It

Day 10: I Sure Will, Pops (12:11 PM)

Father God, thank you for the smile you put on my face today. I will wear it all day long! I know many unnecessary reasons to change what you did, but I refuse to damage our relationship. In Jesus' Name, Amen!

Read James 1:17

Meditation

_____

_____

_____

_____

_____

_____

Release It To Him

_____

_____

_____

_____

_____

_____

_____

_____

_____

_____

_____

_____

_____

_____

Day 11: Claim It (9 AM)

Pops, I'm grateful! Thank you! Today is going to be a good day! In Jesus' Name, Amen!

Read Number 23:19

Meditation

_____

_____

_____

_____

Release It To Him

_____

_____

_____

_____

_____

Day 12: Sooner Than Later (1:06 AM)

Pops, thank you for another day of reflection! I failed in a few areas today, but I'm thankful you gave me another chance! Father, I need you right now! My mind is all over the place about my ex-wife, and I need your strength to let go and believe that you are working on a plan for me just as well as for her! Soon than later, I know the way I feel about life will bring joy rather than pain! In Jesus' Name, Amen!

Read 1 Peter 5:6-10

Meditation

_____

_____

_____

_____

_____

Cast It Unto Him

_____

_____

_____

_____

_____

_____

_____

_____

_____

_____

Day 13: Face Reality (11:24 AM)

Pops, this morning I woke up with the mindset to worship you! My body was tired! My mind was working on overload from anxiety! My thoughts were positioned to please you, but my plan was complete! Thank you for helping me to prioritize my thoughts and actions!

Today father, I need your help to establish the things always to have your space within me clear and prepared to worship you! My place of employment is unorganized! My emotions are unmanaged! The devil continues to try and entice me with things that are not essence anymore. My staff is overwhelmed! My focus from day to day continues to look back and desire stuff you have taken away! I need your guidance right now! I'm trusting you to lead me, guide me, and teach me your ways! In Jesus' Name, Amen!

Read Proverbs 3:3-5

Meditation

_____

_____

_____

_____

_____

Trust Him With It

_____

_____

_____

_____

Day 14: Jesus Loves Me (9 AM)

Father, thank you for loving me the way you do! You continue to help me see the value in my journey through life, my pains, my struggles, my tears, the joy you gave me, and the purpose of every season in this life!

Father, today I need your guidance on listening to your Holy Spirit! Teach me today how to love me! Show me where my focus should be! Help me to execute the plans you have for me!

Father, thanks for an excellent night's rest! Thank you for this peace of mind! Thank you for your time, listening ear, and many blessings today! Thank you, Father, for loving me every day! In Jesus' Name, Amen!

Read James 1:8-9

Meditation

_____

_____

_____

_____

_____

He Is Listening For Your Prayer

_____

_____

_____

_____

_____

_____

_____

_____

<u>Reflection Moment</u>

1. How do you feel now that your prayer life is increasing?

2. Do you see any changes as you travel through life while praying to God?

3. Take what you have learned to embrace the next seven days of your journey to flourish!

Day 15: Keep Moving (10 AM)

Father God, thank you for my experience yesterday and today's mission! My spirit was disturbed by things that I couldn't change. I'm grateful that you allowed me to walk through the pain! Today father, I will keep moving, thriving, serving, and working for you! I know that you will continue to walk with me through my season! In Jesus' Name, Amen!

Read 2 Corinthians 12:7

Meditation

_____

_____

_____

_____

_____

He Is Listening For Your Prayer

_____

_____

_____

_____

_____

_____

_____

_____

Day 16: God Is Working (9 AM)

Father God, thank you for working on me! I understand that your craftsmanship of me is not complete! Today, I believe that! You made me accessible! You set me free! I need your help to understand my freedom! You made me function! I'm ready to function! I need your help to understand the functionality you have for me! You desire me to be focused! I value the essence of being focused! I need your understanding of the things that I need my attend! Show me, father, I'm ready! In Jesus' Name, Amen!

Read John 8:30-33

Meditation

_____

_____

_____

_____

_____

_____

_____

Pray & Leave It There

_____

_____

_____

_____

_____

_____

_____

Day 17: You Told Me, Shown Me, I Believe It (11:49 PM)

Thank you, father, for a power-filled day! I worked hard! I smiled through it all! I did not give up! I thought of past hurts and experiences. I didn't give in to repeating old behavior! I know that I must continue to journey one day at a time. Thank you for telling me that everything is going to be okay! Thank you for showing me that you have me covered! Thank you for reminding me to always believe in you! In Jesus' Name, Amen!

Read 1 Samuel 16:1-3

Meditation

_____

_____

_____

_____

_____

_____

_____

Pray About It

_____

_____

_____

_____

_____

_____

_____

Day 18: Own It (7:56 AM)

Pops, thank you for allowing me to wake up with a smile! Satan tried to drain my energy early this morning! Thanks for keeping me positive and focused! As I plant my feet on the side of my bed, what will you have me do today? In Jesus' Name, Amen!

Read Psalm 30: 1-5

Meditation

_____

_____

_____

He's Listening

_____

_____

_____

_____

_____

Day 19: Get Prepared, Be Prepared (6:31 PM)

Father God, today was a blessing! I was able to rest well! With your strength, I conquered some temptations, prayed to you, and was reminded of my values and worth, as well as realigning my focus towards your glory! Yes, with you, I can do it!

I gave thoughts about my past! I gave a small piece of emotional drainage to my past! With you, I gain a better form of wisdom after releasing those things to you! This evening Pops, I'm ready to close out my day with a smile! I have allowed your Holy Spirit to guide my focus back to the main things of serving you, honoring you, managing my responsibilities, stop dwelling on the past, and I'm ready for you to bless me!

Father, if you don't do anything else for me, I know you have done enough! Help me this evening to finish the essential things. Bless me to love on me! Show me in your word this evening Father, more about your purpose for me! Build-in me a continual peace of mine! Guide my thoughts as I rest this evening! Thank you for a clean and fresh start! In Jesus' Name, Amen!

Read Psalm 51:10

Meditation

_____

_____

_____

_____

_____

_____

Pray Through Having Faith

_____

_____

_____

_____

_____

_____

_____

Day 20: Here I AM (8:17 AM)

Father God, today the first thing that brought joy to my spirit was you! I saw the bright and shiny sun rising! I smiled and rejoiced in this blessing to embrace another day! Right now, I say thank you! Right now, I'm praising you! Right now, I will lift my hands and honor up! Right now, I know that your grace, mercy, love, and Holy Spirit will guide me through today!

Father, I haven't shaved in weeks! I haven't given my best to you! Father, today thank you for a renewed strength to clean up myself and worship you! Thanks for your forgiveness! Thanks for showing me how to forgive! Thanks for blessing me to forgive myself! Thanks for showing me how to forgive others!

Today Pops, I'm ready to lift your Holy name! Nothing else matters! I will allow nothing to stand in the way! I will resist the temptation not to want to give myself away so that you can use me! Father, you are fantastic! You are my Lord and King! It's you who I will follow today! In Jesus' Name, Amen!

Read Isaiah 6:8

Meditation

_____

_____

_____

_____

_____

_____

Talk To Him About It

_____

_____

_____

_____

_____

_____

_____

_____

_____

Day 21: Master It (8:52 AM)

Father God, you are fantastic! Thanks for a powerful weekend! Thanks for everything you've blessed me to use and share with others! This morning pops, I saw an attack that the devil tried to use. Thank you for setting me straight. Father, you know what I need today. Help me to master the things that wanted to destroy me! Help me to remain free from sin! Help me stay alter, sober, and prepared to journey today, honoring your purpose for me! In Jesus' Name, Amen!

Read Genesis 4:6-7

Meditation

_____

_____

_____

_____

_____

_____

Faithful Prayers Makes & Impact

_____

_____

_____

_____

_____

_____

_____

_____

<u>Reflection Moments</u>

1. What's your defining moment that God has revealed to you this past week?

2. How will you use this reflection of you to be a better person?

3. Take what you have learned to embrace the next seven days of your journey to excel!

Day 22: Love On You (12:24 AM)

Dear Father,

Today was awesome! Thank you! I love you, and I know you love me! Thanks for the confirmation of joy, peace, and abundant life! In Jesus' Name, Amen!

Read Psalm 1:1-6

Meditation

_____

_____

_____

Praise Him

_____

_____

_____

Day 23: Remain Calm (8:45 AM)

Dear Father, I woke up this morning with a smile! Thank you! I praise you! I honor you! I'm happy to call you, my Father! Today is going to be a great day! Please, Father, bless everyone across the world today! Help us to see your glory, purpose, and mission! Help us to travel through today following your instructions! In Jesus' Name, Amen!

Read 1 Thessalonians 5:16-18

Meditation

_____

_____

_____

_____

_____

_____

Pray To The Father

_____

_____

_____

_____

_____

_____

_____

_____

Day 24: Step Into Your Future (9:11 AM)

Father God, I need you right now to channel my focus on what's right! My emotions are trying to drive me into wanting what you have taken away. I miss being married! I miss providing for the wife I had! I miss nurturing in a marriage! I miss all the benefits of being married! Father, I see a new purpose! It's in you! I've learned many things during my marriage, in the separation, and after the divorce!

Father, today I see that you have placed me in a new future. Please, Father, protect my heart! Show me how to guard it! Produce in me a positive mindset! Guide me towards a greater purpose! Bless me to never forget my experiences within you! In Jesus Christ's Name, Amen!

(11:31 AM)

Father God, help me to stop going back! You blessed me with a clean slate! You gave me a fresh start! You freed me from the bondage of long-term destruction! I need your help to embrace the newness of my future. Why? Because you love me, and you told me that you would never leave me nor for-sake me! You said that you'd provide for me! You said you told me to ask, and I will receive it! Father, I ask that you keep guiding me towards you! Prepare me for my future! In Jesus' Name, Amen!

Read Psalm 51:10

Meditation

_____

_____

_____

_____

_____

_____

Believe He Will Answer In Due Time

_____

_____

_____

_____

_____

_____

_____

_____

Day 25: Chose To Move Forward (5:10 AM)

Father, I get it! In Jesus' Name, Amen!

Read 1 Samuel 16:1-3

Meditation

_____

_____

_____

_____

Pray With Active Faith

_____

_____

_____

_____

_____

Day 26: Celebrate (12:11 AM)

Father God, thanks for blessing me with another year of life! I know you have plans for me and my future! I'm ready for the itinerary! In Jesus' Name, Amen!

Read John 15:7

Meditation

_____

_____

_____

Pray With Joy

_____

_____

_____

_____

Day 27: Build Up, Don't Tear Down (7:21 AM)

Dear Father, thank you! Yesterday was amazing! You blessed me to keep smiling! You gave me a healthy path to follow! You introduced me to a beautiful woman! You strengthen me to keep moving through the course of my past, pains, emotional strains, thoughts of failure, ideas of shame, regrets, and thoughts that I believed would never change, father. I'm excited but not anxious!

Today Father, I'm going to worship you in spirit and in truth! I'm trusting you and your ways! I'm seeking you! I'm going to tell someone about you! I'm proud to call you, my pops!

Thanks, pops, for listening, understanding, and answering my prayers! I know that you love me! I understand how you never left me, nor have you forgotten about me! Thank You! Father, prepare my heart, mind, body, and soul to demonstrate what your plans are for me! In Jesus Christ, Name, Amen!

Read Deuteronomy 31:6, 8; Hebrews 13:5, Isaiah 41:10-13

Meditation

_____

_____

_____

_____

_____

Pray With Joy

_____

_____

_____

_____

_____

_____

_____

Day 28: Look Back & Tell God Thank You (7:06 AM)

Father God, our twenty-eight-day journey through February was beautiful! I learned a lot! I embraced your plans for me! I failed short a few times! You gave me opportunities to make a difference! You answered a few of my prayers. You told me No on a few things! Some things that I asked for you told me to wait! On day twenty-eight, I look back and simply say thank you! In Jesus' Name, Amen!

Read Hebrews 12:11

Meditation

_____

_____

_____

_____

_____

_____

Pray With Understanding

_____

_____

_____

_____

_____

_____

_____

<u>Reflection Moments</u>

1. Do not experience unnecessary setbacks if you do not have to!

2. Do not be afraid to pray about everything!

3. Take what you have learned to embrace the next seven days of your journey to accomplish God's plan for you!

Day 29; Start Today, Not Tomorrow (12:54 AM)

Father, God, once again, I say thanks! In Jesus' Name, Amen!

Read Matthew 22:37-40

Meditation

_____

_____

_____

_____

Pray About It

_____

_____

_____

_____

_____

_____

Day 30; I Can Handle It (9:53 AM)

Father, God, you have blessed me beyond measure! Thank you! Today, I'm starting with the expression of a humble spirit, ready to embrace my next scheduled season!

This past week pops, my faith was tested! Emotionally I feel better! Physically I feel stronger! Mentally I feel braver! Spiritually I think your power continues to push me towards new adventures in chapter thirty-one of my life!

Women have reached out to me! The functionality and distractions in my workplace are trying to break me! My family continues to encourage me! Performing in ministry is where I want to be! You, Father, have not stop guiding me!

As I better understand all the new tools, resources, vision, mission, and perspective that you gave me, please, father, help me to handle everything appropriately! I'm not going to give up! I'm not planning to give in to problems, troubles, emotional strains, fears, or setbacks! Today pops, help me to understand the instructions for my new chapter! In Jesus' Name, Amen!

Read Phil. 2:2-6; Romans 14:15; 15:1

Meditation

_____

_____

_____

_____

_____

_____

Pray For God's Wisdom

_____

_____

_____

_____

_____

_____

_____

Day 31; Let Him Empower You (4:30 PM)

Father God, today started rocky! My mind was traveling in multiple directions at the same time! My focus was on yesterday, today, and tomorrow! The job functions captured my energy! Being single again distractions me! Trying not to deal with conflicts, challenges, and stress correctly attacked my faith that's positioned to please you! Worship was refreshing! Visitors that stopped by were enlightening! The new level, season, and environment of my journey help me relax my emotions! Father, I'm grateful for what's about to happen during this chapter of my life. In Jesus' Name, Amen!

Read Ephesians 4:29-31

Meditation

_____

_____

_____

_____

_____

_____

Pray For Understanding

_____

_____

_____

_____

_____

_____

_____

_____

Day 32; Create New Memories (8:26 AM)

Father God, I awake with a smile and a focus that you gave me! Why? Because at that moment, I further understood that you had a mission for me today! Help me to create better memories today! Show me how to embrace the experience for new memories! Guide me to live with new memories! Teach me the process of how memories work! Afford me the strength and energy to demonstrate positive focus and vanquish dead memories! Bless me today, father, to deal with today and create new memories! In Jesus' Name, Amen!

Read Psalm 100:1-5

Meditation

_____

_____

_____

_____

_____

_____

Pray

_____

_____

_____

_____

_____

_____

_____

_____

Day 33; Know Your Heart (6:55 AM)

Good Morning Father! At this hour, my mind is filled with joy and anxiety simultaneously. I know you created me for a purpose, and I can't allow anyone to scare me into the unbelief of you walking with me. Right now, pops; I'm worried about my job, the people, the workload, and my work peers. I know that everything works together for your finished product to be presented in its timing as great, fantastic, and wonderful. Like your product, I need you to help me simply let go of the fear and pick up your power, love, and sound mind. In Jesus' Name, Amen!

Read John 17:14-16; 2 Tim. 1:7

Meditation

_____

_____

_____

_____

_____

_____

Pray

_____

_____

_____

_____

_____

_____

_____

_____

_____

Day 34; Why Should I Feel Discouraged (9:37 PM)

Pops, today was awesome! I push through a limit by stepping on Faith and asking for help! I helped produce the necessary products for service! I expressed my feelings and thoughts for essential support as a Director! I said I was sorry a few times! I didn't allow the devil to win! I shared with my Church Family a few details about your journey for me! I left work at work! I planned out how you want me to use your money! Father, I'm grateful for the experience, exposure, and exercise of today's challenges! I understand it's not essential to prioritize or ponder the essence of being discouraged! I'm ready for the next phase of my journey! In Jesus' Name, Amen!

Read Matthew 7:7-8

Meditation

_____

_____

_____

_____

Pray

_____

_____

_____

_____

_____

_____

_____

_____

_____

_____

Day 35; The Foundation (6:05 AM)

Good Morning, Father! I know today is going to be phenomenal! You woke me up! You gave me the energy to move! You reminded me that I'm not alone! My faith is stable and prepared to please you today! Despite the circumstances of being short-staffed and feeling drained physically, I know the established foundation with you is solid. In Jesus' Name, Amen!

Read Matthew 16: 33; Hebrews 4:15-16

Meditation

_____

_____

_____

_____

_____

_____

Pray

_____

_____

_____

_____

_____

_____

_____

_____

<u>Reflection Moments</u>

1.   After a full thirty plus days of prayer how do you feel?

2.   Do not stop interceding prayers for other!

3.   Prepare for your change to come!

Day 36; Keep It 100 (8:12 AM)

Good Morning, Pops! I remember asking for a role as a Director of Culinary! Man, the challenges are real. Today, someone called out! I'm still behind on my weekly tasks! I'm ready for an uninterrupted day off! My staff is feeling drained! My resource support, I don't know what to say! Today, I need a boost, not to walk away from your blessings. In Jesus' Name, Amen!

Read 1 Peter 5:6-7

Day 38; Confident (10:35PM)

Father God today was amazing! I preached your word! I used your examples! I stated your facts! I simply gave you the keys to drive the focus of my day! I'm grateful for the interview of a potential father-in-law. I smiled at the sight of how you are working and paving the way towards husband hood! I'm thankful for your blessing of walking through today with my current staffing challenges, physically being tired, and a small conversation with a new friend that you sent my way! Thanks for a beautiful weekend! I'm glad I used your time to clean my home! I appreciate you guiding me to save more money, make better decisions, and keep it accurate and straightforward! In Jesus' Name, Amen!

Read Joshua 24:15

Meditation

_____

_____

_____

_____

_____

_____

_____

Pray

_____

_____

_____

_____

_____

_____

_____

Day 39; Blessed (10:05 PM)

Pops not only today was a good day; you blessed me more than I deserve! You showed me how to take care of what's priority! You strengthen me to go the extra mile! You allowed me to exercise the essence to say no to SIN! You gave me a passion for demonstrating compassion! You helped me to understand the power of listening! You monitor my behaviors, and I trust they are pleasing to you! My team was blessed! My focus for today was intact! Thank you for trusting me with your blessings! In Jesus' Name, Amen!

Read James 1:25

Meditation

_____

_____

_____

_____

_____

Pray

_____

_____

_____

_____

_____

_____

_____

_____

Day 40; Peace To Keep Pushing (10:10 PM)

Good Evening Pops! Today was great! You blessed my operation with two interviews! We trust that both will work out! You gave my team and me the proper strength and focus to keep pushing despite unexpected Ice Cream issues! You blessed the lunch and dinner hours! You showed up with the plan for us to follow! Pops, you did it! We are grateful!

There was a minor issue with the attitude approach of one of the helpers! Please, father, guide their spirit! The team you gave me doesn't need drama! Today, Father, my lead cook, obtained more peace to perform at the optimum level! One of my team members was blessed, recognized, and rewarded! Today's operation was managed smoothly! I found peace to keep pushing because you are driving! In Jesus' Name, Amen!

Read I Thessalonians 4:1

Meditation

_____

_____

_____

_____

_____

_____

_____

Pray

_____

_____

_____

_____

_____

_____

_____

_____

Day 41; Focused (6:21 AM)

Good Morning Pops! Thanks for waking me up to start another day refreshed and prepared for action! Bless me with the zeal to remain on track! Guide my team to keep things intact! Channel the focus of my support team/visitors today! Comfort our residents and staff to create an exceptional experience for one another! I'm glad that I started my day with devotion to you! You reminded me how you made everything, and everything belongs to you! My focus is on the performance of how you will use me today as one of your creations! In Jesus' Name, Amen!

Read Colossians 1:15-16

Meditation

_____

_____

_____

_____

_____

_____

Pray

_____

_____

_____

_____

_____

_____

_____

_____

Day 42; Remain Through The Transition (10:25 AM)

Thank You, Father! Thank You, Jesus! Thank You, Holy Spirit! In Jesus' Name, Amen!

Read Psalm 95:1-3

Meditation

_____

_____

_____

_____

_____

Pray

_____

_____

_____

_____

_____

Reflection Moments

1. List three changes that occurred as you continued to pray about everything!

    A. _____

    B. _____

    C. _____

2. What will you continue to do as you keep a solid connection with the creator in prayer?

3. Always trust God's process, timing, and purpose for you!

Day 43; It's God's Transition, Not Mine! (7:45 AM)

Good Morning Father! I felt great this morning! I woke up to what I expected from you. I thought about my past and didn't act on it! I feel refreshed, and I'm grateful for the renewed strength! I'm ready for the challenges of today, and I know that you are with me! My great-grandmother often reminds me that you are all that I need. Now that doesn't negate my desire to marry again! I know pops in your perfect time you will allow me to find her loving you than anything and above everything, working for you, serving you, ready to be committed to one marital union, that woman who is beautiful inside-out, and who will journey through life with me while managing the attacks that don't desire to see a happy/healthy couple!

Today pops, I don't know what I'm walking into at my place of employment! Thanks for reminding me to remain calm/humble and allow you to do your thang with the issues that are out of my control. Please, father, guide the intent and motive of the toxic events that occurred within the past two days. You know what you're doing, and I appreciate your reminding me of my position to do the right thing!

Bless my team, the operation, the focus, the scheduled events, and the workload to be practical. Please help my leadership team and me to work together more intelligently, not harder, and with confidence to manage our responsibilities! I know you have a plan! It's your transition, and I'm glad you find me worthy of being a part of the results! In Jesus' Name, Amen!

Read Psalm 69:30

Meditation

_____

_____

_____

_____

_____

What's Your Prayer

_____

_____

_____

_____

_____

_____

_____

Day 44; He Paid It All (12:25 AM)

Thanks, Pop! In Jesus' Name, Amen!

Read Isaiah 53:7

Meditation

_____

_____

_____

Pray To Him

_____

_____

_____

_____

_____

_____

_____

Day 45; That Was Different (8:24 AM)

Good Morning Pops! My heart, mind, body, and soul are filled with joy! Yesterday was beautiful, but today is going to be awesome! Last week was great, but this week will be phenomenal! Pops, thank you for a good day off yesterday and a prepared one for the day! Please, father, strengthen my operation of employment! Comfort the hearts of my staff and residents! Bless your Christian to worship you in spirit and with an honest heart!

I am glad you changed my condition of who I used to be! I am grateful for the new position of thriving within doing what's right, making good mistakes, not bad ones, and for keeping my focus on you! Father, I'm learning every day to lean on you! Every day I'm learning more to trust you! Every day I'm learning to demonstrate faith that pleases you!

Today Pops is different because you changed my condition of worrying, lying, depression, wondering, and so much more towards the action to be different! This new position feels good! My mind is at peace! My heart is yours! You properly guide my spirit! You help me to discipline my body! My soul belongs to you! In Jesus Christ's Name, Amen!

Read Psalm 18:1-3

Meditation

Pray To Him

Day 46; Emotional Adrenaline (11 PM)

Pops, today was tuff mentally! Thank you for walking me through and learning from a repeated exercise. In Jesus' Name, Amen!

Read II Cor. 12:5-6

Meditation

_____

_____

_____

_____

Pray To Him

_____

_____

_____

_____

_____

Day 47; Emotional Drainage (10:09PM)

Pops, today was great! I experienced a lot with staffing on my job! I cried out to you about my frustrations over my marriage ending in divorce! You sent blessings to my organization, with three new hires starting simultaneously! You gave me an allowance to celebrate my team! You strengthen me to be an example in another role in my operation! I cried out to you more about the things that bothered me yesterday, and I'm grateful that things are getting better daily! Father, I want to say and do more, but I'm currently emotionally drained! I know you are working on a plan! Pops, I want to be near you every day! In Jesus' Name, Amen!

Read Psalm 4:1-8

Meditation

_____

_____

_____

_____

_____

_____

_____

Pour Out Yourself To Him

_____

_____

_____

_____

_____

_____

_____

Day 48; I Know You Understanding (9:07 PM)

Father God, today was amazing! I felt anxiety about the thoughts of my past marriage, ole/new pains, rejection, grief, pride, and much more that's become easier to manage! Pops, I waited for a response from what was unwilling, and I appreciate you for pushing me to keep moving through my valley! I know you understand my journey, struggles, stress, challenges, and passions! Thank you for blessing me to arrive at your blessed response to keep my head high!

Today, Father, you gave me comfort and peace to smile! I realize how I contributed to my painful, repeated exercises. They were unnecessary! You already conquered the battle for me! You already gave me a new direction! You already structured my focus! You already asked me to stop wasting time and continue being about your business!

I see the pathway to better days! I know the path to a better future! I see the way to joining a faithful, committed, loving, submissive, and authentic wife in the future! I see a sustainable and flexible career in my future! I see children in my future! I see more thriving in ministry! I see a home in my future! I see myself and my family happy, healthy, and fruitful in our future! Thanks, pops, for allowing me to understand your plans! I don't know your timing, but I know you got me! You got us! In Jesus' Name, Amen!

Read Psalm 9:1-4

Meditation

_____

_____

_____

_____

_____

_____

He's Listening

_____

_____

_____

_____

_____

_____

_____

_____

Day 49; You vs. You (12:53 PM)

Father God, I realized something today! It's me verse me! It's not a matter of how successful a person, place, or substance may appear; it's you and me on this journey together! As I mentioned last night, I'm grateful for what you added to my journey as I continue seeking you and what's being crafted just for me. You continue to show me how much you love me! You already gave me more than what I need! You are already in front of my dark valleys! I must stop worrying about what doesn't exist anymore!

Father, I understand a little more about how you're turning my grief into glory! I feel the weight of depression, stress, complacency, and fear being lifted! I value my relationship with you as my father, provider, protector, guide, and corrector! Pops, I realize I need help dealing with me! In Jesus' Name, Amen!

Read Deuteronomy 31:6

Meditation

_____

_____

_____

Let Him Help You

_____

_____

_____

_____

_____

<u>Reflection Moments</u>

1. Do you feel the difference prayer creates in you to relax and trust God?

2. Always use your prayer line with the creator for everything!

3. Do not try to do life without God's strength, resources, and guidance!

Day 50; That's My Zeal (10:22 PM)

Father God, at this moment, I'm content! Worry conquered me yesterday. You told me not to worry! It's not essential to worry! Why worry! Worrying does not bring justice or peace! Worry defeats! Thank for pops for relaxing my mind to keep moving forward through the pain! You gave me the zeal to flourish and be honest! Help me rekindle, rebuild, demonstrate, and thrive within the crafted enthusiasm you gave me! In Jesus' Name, Amen!

Read Philippians 4:6-13

Meditation

Let Him Help You

Day 51: Enough Said (6:44 AM)

Pops, yesterday was quite interesting! I'm grateful for you allowing me to be in attendance to give support, show support, and be blessed to share the talents that you've given me! The attacks from the devil tried their best to pull my spirit down, but your strength in me defeated the pressure!

I wanted to give up a couple of times, but you positioned my head and shoulders to hang high! I didn't overeat! I exercised! I got some rest the night before! My past habit didn't conquer me! You gave me a refreshed mindset! Pops, I'm grateful! I'm still standing, walking, and thriving through the pain! In Jesus' Name, Amen!

Read 1 Corinthians 15:58

Meditation

_____

_____

_____

_____

_____

Let Him Guide You

_____

_____

_____

_____

_____

_____

_____

Day 52: I See You (4:25 PM)

Father God, you are who I need! Yesterday was incredible, but today in words, I cannot explain! I truly enjoyed your outings for me to have advertised my literature masterpieces and attended the comedy/concert to see The Mann Family. My heart is at peace! My mind continues to learn and cultivate what's essential! My soul is protected! My body continues through healthy development while under subjection! Pops, I'm glad you used me to help many today!

One of my mentees was empowered today! One of my sisters purchased a copy of book number one! I prayed for my family, Journey, and future! I preached your word! Some stated they enjoyed your message! At this moment, I see your work through me!

Pops, I see more clearly why you have me on this path. A path of expansion and development. You sent me away from my biological family, gave me more ministry endeavors, and made me a Director of Culinary, I'm embracing the essence of being a faithful divorcee, and you assigned me to be an Assistant Minister & Youth Director, God, I see you working on my future! Thank You! In Jesus' Name, Amen!

Read 1 Peter 5:6-10

Meditation

_____

_____

_____

_____

_____

Pray

_____

_____

_____

_____

_____

_____

_____

Day 53; Polish Me Father (11:19 PM)

In Jesus' Name, Amen!

Read Psalm 119:59

Meditation

_____

_____

_____

_____

_____

Cast It

_____

_____

_____

_____

_____

Day 54; Smile and Keep Thriving (7:38 AM)

Good Morning Pops! Thank you for a peaceful night's rest! Thank you for allowing me to see you another day. Thank you for the blessing to function without any physical assistance from others! Thank you for good health, strength, and purpose! Thank you, father, for a job, career, transportation, savings, and a future! Father, I wake up with a bit of worry on my mind, but you reminded me to smile and keep thriving! I know today is going to be a good day! In Jesus' Name, Amen!

Read Psalm 18:1-3

Meditation

_____

_____

_____

_____

_____

_____

Cast It

_____

_____

_____

_____

_____

_____

_____

_____

_____

Day 55; Be Honest (7:43 AM)

Good Morning Father! I read something this morning that helped me further understand proper energy expansion. Since 2020, experiencing separation in marriage, after the loss of my father in 2021, receiving the news that one of my young cousins was killed, and traveling a journey through divorce, I'm still trying to find structure in some areas. I understand that my journey is a marathon and not a Sprint.

Father, I feel my energy has expanded in more places than in some. At the start of 2021, you gave me a focus to stop some bad, negative, and sinful habits! January was no Masturbation from missing sexual carvings after divorce! February was twenty-eight days of prayer, exercise, and plenty of water daily! March was thirty to sixty minutes with you, Father, less sweets, and for resting well at night! April was assigned to repeat the first quarter! As I March towards May, I'm ready for your new journey for me!

I'm ready for good challenges, transformed worries into worship, a step toward the future you have planned for me, and a peace past my understanding! Father, thank you for reminding me that we are braver, stronger, and more innovative through you and by the experiences we've encountered with you! As you prepare me for my future, I'm thankful, to be honest! I'm human in flesh and spirit as my identity of being your child by transforming my mindset daily! I'm Jesus Name, Amen!

Read Joshua 1:9

Meditation

_____

_____

_____

_____

_____

_____

Cast It

_____

_____

_____

_____

_____

_____

_____

_____

Day 56; Laugh (11:36 PM)

Good Evening Father! Today was nothing below powerful! I felt my worries fade away! I internalized and gained the value of more details for my new journey! I spoke to my past hurts and continued to press forward! I saw the devil's schemes that were ready to attack me! Father, I trust that you got me!

As I laugh at myself through myself, I'm grateful for my relationship with you. No, I don't want to be without a spouse forever, and I appreciate your company! No, I don't want to grieve over the nouns that spoke to my past/present pains forever! I don't want to resort back to what did not work, the aspects that hindered my growth, or a mindset of complacency.

Pops, I laugh because I'm content with the new perspective you gave me! I'm free to live respectfully! I am glad to be positioned to thrive in everything you expect through me! It feels good to laugh! In Jesus' Name, Amen!

Read Psalm 30:11; Job 8:21; Psalm 126:2

Meditation

_____

_____

_____

_____

_____

_____

_____

Cast It

_____

_____

_____

_____

_____

_____

_____

_____

<u>Reflection Moments</u>

1. You're on a role with your prayer life! How can you help someone else to create and sustain a healthy prayer life with the creator?

2. Remember that God did not place you here to worry! Cast it to him!

3. Believe and trust the ultimate catalyst!

Day 57; Don't Be Surprised (3:59 PM)

What's up, Pops? Today has been quite interesting! You allowed me to experience a new defining moment. I didn't expect it! I didn't see it coming! I'm humbled! To have heard, read, and be dismissed from a work site! I wanted to cry, but you didn't allow me! I wanted to become angry, but you stopped me! I wanted to throw a temper tantrum, but you surprised me with joy multiplied with peace!

Thank you, Pops, for my experiences of not burning bridges. I'm grateful for the surprise! The reconnection and recommendations humble me! You know what I need for my next season! You know what's in the oven for me! I'm ready for the next steps! In Jesus' Name, Amen!

Read Proverbs 15:13; 15:15; 17:22

Meditation

_____

_____

_____

_____

_____

_____

_____

Pray

_____

_____

_____

_____

_____

_____

Day 58; Deliverance Is Coming (2:09PM)

Good Afternoon, Father! Today started wonderfully! At this moment, it has excelled too excellent! This morning a little after 8 AM, you sent me an email to respond to quickly! We replied expeditiously! At 2:09 PM, we parked in the parking lot of our potential new employer! Pops, I'm humbled!

Thank you for blessing me with the energy to clean your building! Thanks for a mindset that is content in my current circumstances! Thanks for blessing me to remain active and focused on your mission for me! Thanks for blessing me to manage my stressors that are consistently transforming into joy! Pops, thank you for helping me thrive in areas I never imagined!

I know, Father, that your deliverance process is effective, on time, and scheduled to allow me to embrace your abundant future! Please, Father, bless everyone on their journey through life despite the coming challenges. To you, my friends, loved ones, or family members, deliverance is coming! In Jesus' Name, Amen!

Read Psalm 32:7

Meditation

Pray

Final Exam

T/F God has forgotten about you!

T/F You will not overcome your fears!

T/F A healthy prayer life is essential!

T/F My problems control me!

T/F God can help manage my habits and troubles!

T/F Building a solid connection with God helped me during this 58-day journey!

T/F I'm prepared to worry less!

T/F I will continue to pray about everything to God!

ABOUT THE AUTHOR

Maurice Schofield is a prolific culinary professional, author, and communicator. He is noted for his authentic approach in ministry work, culinary expertise, and mentorship abilities. Maurice was produced in an environment that centers family, Christian values, and unconditional love. He has a testimony to share of various endured struggles, challenges, and conquered fears. Through every work and life experience he has acquired more tools to demonstrate service for the community and his family.

Maurice is a committed leader in helping others achieve their greatest form of excellence one step at a time. He has obtained an Associate of Science in Business Administration, a Bachelor of Science in Religious Education, and a Master of Science in Human Services from Amridge University. He is currently the Assistant Minister & Youth Director at the Eastside Church of Christ in Lee's Summit, Missouri. His continual mission is to help fortify families across the world by winning souls for Christ Jesus.

Other books by Maurice Schofield:

"Becoming Approachable"

Crafted to motivate Parents,
Children, and Christians to
thrive in their approach with
others!

"Damaged Not Destroyed"

Crafted to empower Children, Parents, and New Christians to excel in life!

"The Path To Spiritual Purpose"

Crafted to inspire Children, Families, and Christians on their journey with God!

Please reach out for more information, details, or to order your signature copy today!

Mauriceschofield65@gmail.com

(904) 662-5520

Made in the USA
Middletown, DE
10 November 2022

14381568R00090